This book belongs to:

....

....

Written by Kath Smith
Illustrated by Caroline Jayne Church
Designed by Andrea Newton
Language consultant: Betty Root

This is a Parragon book
This edition published in 2005

Parragon
Queen Street House
4 Queen Street
Bath, BA1 1HE, UK

p

Knights are Brave

Shy Sir
MacEye

Although a good knight, Sir MacEye
was really rather shy.
When anybody spoke to him,
he'd blush and not reply.

He dreaded meeting strangers.
If someone came to call ...
he'd raise the drawbridge in a flash
and hide behind a wall.

When asked to go to parties
(he wished it wasn't so),
he'd get so very nervous
and just refuse to go!

He longed to talk to Princess Poll,
but every time he tried,
with knocking knees and pounding heart,
he'd find himself tongue-tied.

"Faint heart never won a lady!"
confided Fairy Heather.
"I have a plan to help you out.
I've thought of something clever!

Today there is a royal joust.
The winner gets a prize
from Princess Polly's hands, you know.
That's where the answer lies!"

9

Every knight arrived at noon
to play the jousting game –
including one mysterious chap,
a knight who had no name!

His armour was as black as night,
his horse was snowy white.
This *mystery* knight won every charge –
a truly noble sight!

A whisper ran around the crowd.
"Who can he be?" they said.
Princess Polly longed to know.
She sighed and scratched her head.

The knight knelt down upon the steps
and lifted his disguise.
"It's Sir MacEye!" the princess cried.
"I can't believe my eyes!"

"I usually feel shy," he said.
"But when I wear this mask,
I feel I can do anything,
and even dare to ask...

if you would come to tea with me,"
he finished in a rush.
"I'd love to come," the princess smiled
and answered with a blush.

Brave Sir Dave

Sir Dave was the most dashing knight
to serve the king and queen.
He carried out the bravest deeds
that you have ever seen.

If someone needed rescuing,
if dragons were about,
Sir Dave was always on the spot
to sort the trouble out.

He never seemed to be afraid,
and nothing made him quiver.
Just one mention of his name
would make a dragon shiver!

The trouble was the other knights
never got to try.
Sir Dave was always on the scene ...
"MIND OUT! JUST LET ME BY!"

One day, Dave was just too eager.
He rescued a princess
when calmly playing on her own.
She wasn't in distress!

"It would be nice," sighed Sir MacEye,
"if we could help out, too,
performing some heroic deeds
the way knights ought to do!"

Then one day, unexpectedly,
the others got their call
to rescue brave Sir Dave at once.
"I'm stuck up on this wall!

I'm trapped!" he cried. "I cannot move!
The problem is, you see …
there is a GREAT BIG SPIDER
right here in front of me!"

The other knights knew what to do,
(for knights are good that way).
"We'll catch it in a goblet –
we'll act without delay!"

Soon the furry thing was gone.
Dave climbed down off the wall.
"How brave you are," he told his friends.
"I want to thank you all.

I've learned my lesson well," he said.
"Though brave as I can be ...
everyone needs help sometimes
– including even ME!"

Messy Sir Jessie

Sir Jessie was a gentle chap,
honest, brave and true.
He always acted in the way
a good knight ought to do.

The problem was the other knights
did not like Sir Jessie.
"Call himself a noble knight?
He always looks so messy!"

Whenever there's a meeting
of royal knights he's late.
He turns up half way through the day ...
and in a dreadful state.

"You look a fright!" cried Sir MacEye.
"It really is not right.
We can't allow a scruffy tramp
to be a royal knight!

Your chain mail is all rusty.
Your hair is full of straw.
Your clothes are creased. It looks as if
you slept upon the floor!"

Brave Sir Dave spoke for the rest.
"This is a final warning!
You'd better turn up spick and span
for jousting in the morning."

But though he tried his very best
to be there right on time,
Jessie turned up late again,
just as the clock struck nine.

"What a sight!" cried brave Sir Dave.
"He really has to go!
It looks as if he dipped himself
in mud from head to toe!"

"Excuse me!" Princess Susie said.
"I have Sir Jessie's shield.
He dropped it as he caught the bull
that chased me in the field.

He's always helping everyone.
He has a kindly heart!
He truly is a noble knight
although his clothes aren't smart!"

The other knights bowed their heads.
"How wrong we were," they said.
"It's not about the way you look
but what you DO instead!"